Sheila Kanwal was born on the 31 May 1931 in North India in a state called Punjab. She received her education in Christian schools and colleges and finished her education with a BABT degree. She then taught in the same high school where she did her schooling.

In 1963, she had the opportunity to come to Britain to teach. She found a position in a higher secondary school, where she stayed for twenty-three years, teaching humanities. She was given the responsibility to take charge of the religious education throughout the school, which she did for seventeen years.

She loves telling stories and *Donkey the Beast of Burden* is one example.

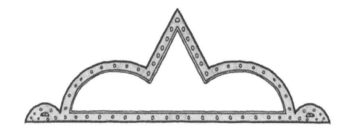

DONKEY
THE BEAST OF BURDEN

DONKEY
THE BEAST OF BURDEN

Sheila Kanwal

ATHENA PRESS

LONDON

ISBN 978 1 84748 355 3

First published 2008
ATHENA PRESS
Queen's House, 2 Holly Road
Twickenham TW1 4EG
United Kingdom

Printed for Athena Press

Do you know what the phrase
'Beast of Burden' means?

Yes, you are right –
animals that carry a burden or
heavy load.

Can you name a few beasts
of burden?

Well, I will give you a clue.

This animal has two big ears, four fat legs and a **very** fat nose.

His nose is also called a 'Trunk'.

Yes, you got it, it's an elephant.

Can you name more beasts of burden?

Look at the picture on top and on the opposite page.

You are right, horses, mules, camels and...

donkeys!

Our story is about
a donkey, who
belonged to a
merchant.

This merchant lived
in an Indian village
called Saudagar
Nagar.

Saudagar Nagar
means 'the abode of
the merchants'.

The donkey was called Khushia, which means 'Happy'.

But actually Khushia was not happy at all.

His master was a very hard taskmaster indeed.

He made him work long hours
and gave him no love or care.

Khushia was sad;
he did not know what to do with himself

He had tried very hard to please his master
by carrying more burden,
but nothing seemed to please him.

Khushia became more and more sad.
His health soon began to show the stresses
and strains of heavy routine.

It just so happened that there lived another donkey in the same village.

His name was Munshi.

One day Munshi saw Khushia on one of his rounds – he asked him about his life and his work.

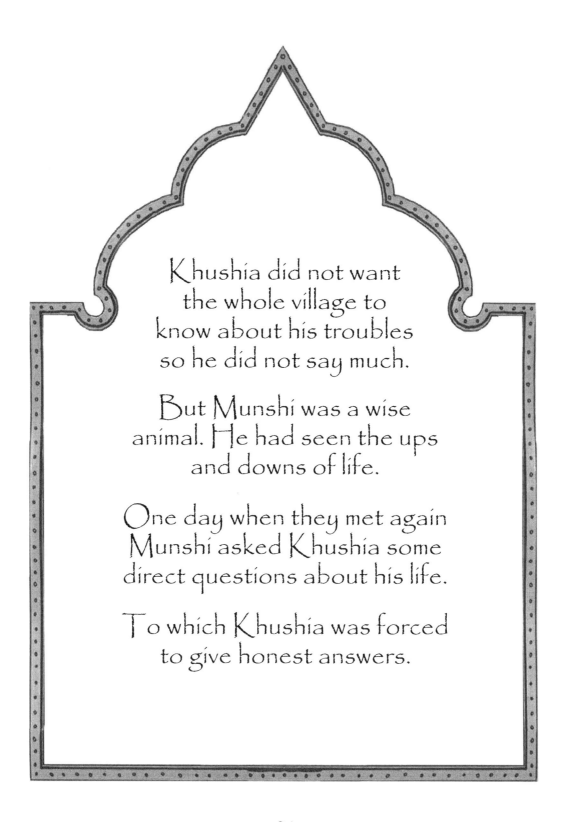

Khushia did not want
the whole village to
know about his troubles
so he did not say much.

But Munshi was a wise
animal. He had seen the ups
and downs of life.

One day when they met again
Munshi asked Khushia some
direct questions about his life.

To which Khushia was forced
to give honest answers.

Khushia said to Munshi,

'Sir, I am sorry to say that inspite of my
honest dealings with my master,
he has treated me very unkindly.

'To tell you the truth, I am sick and
tired of my life.

'My master deals in rock salt and
he makes me work the whole day long.
I carry heavy sacks of salt ten miles to
the other side of the stream,
and I tell you it is no laughing matter.

'This hard and heavy burden has broken my back, my legs tremble when I walk and I get out of breath. I have even blacked out once or twice.'

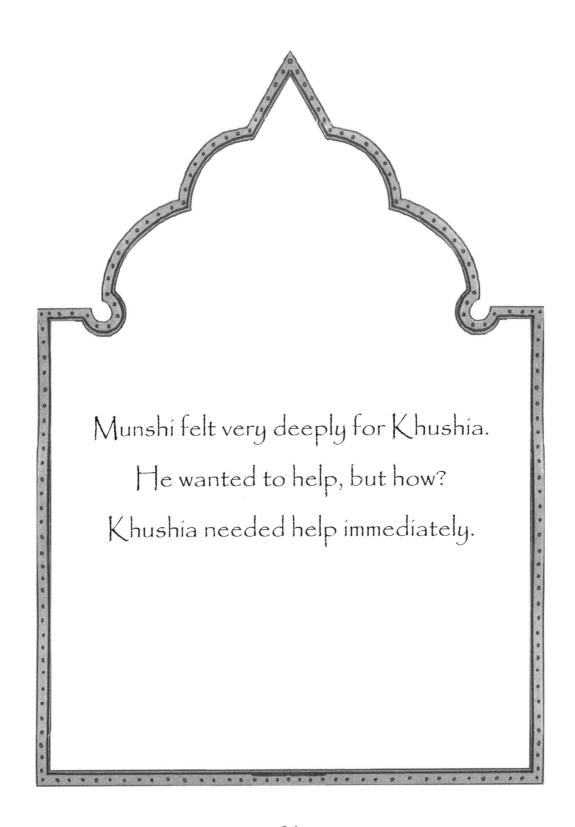

Munshi felt very deeply for Khushia.

He wanted to help, but how?

Khushia needed help immediately.

Munshi felt no sympathy for the merchant. He wanted to teach such a mean person a good lesson.

Munshi thought for a moment, then he began to speak to Khushia very quietly in his ear, in a very serious manner.

'Listen, Khushia,' said Munshi in a thoughtful manner.

'Tomorrow, when you carry your burden to the other side of the stream, do not go through the shallow water.

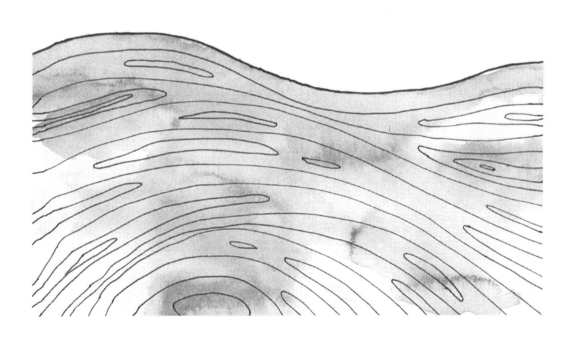

Cross the stream where the water is deep.
Let the sacks stay in the water for some time.'

The next day, Khushia went to his master's door as usual and waited there patiently.

His master brought out two heavy sacks of rock salt and placed them on Khushia's sore back.

28

As Khushia walked towards the stream, Munshi's words rang loudly in his mind and as he drew closer to the water his mind became full of hatred for his master, who had treated him so harshly.

'Go through the deep waters.'

'Go through the deep waters.'

Khushia imagined Munshi standing at the edge of the stream, ordering him to go through the deep waters.

Khushia directed himself toward the deep waters and he swam towards the deeper depths. The sacks were gradually covered by the waves. Khushia felt happy; his sore back no longer felt painful. He swam to the other side with ease.

Khushia stood proudly on the dry land. He felt strongly pleased with what he had done

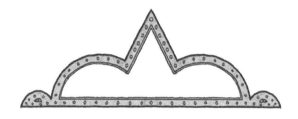

His burden was no longer as heavy as it had seemed before he had entered the stream.

A considerable amount of salt had been washed away by the river.

This went on for some time.

The merchant began
to lose money.

One day he followed
Khushia quietly,
keeping a good
distance between
Khushia and himself.

Khushia went to the stream as usual. He looked for the deep water and plunged himself into the stream without a thought.

The merchant could not believe his eyes. He was mad with rage.

'I will teach this rascal a lesson! A lesson he will remember to his dying day!'

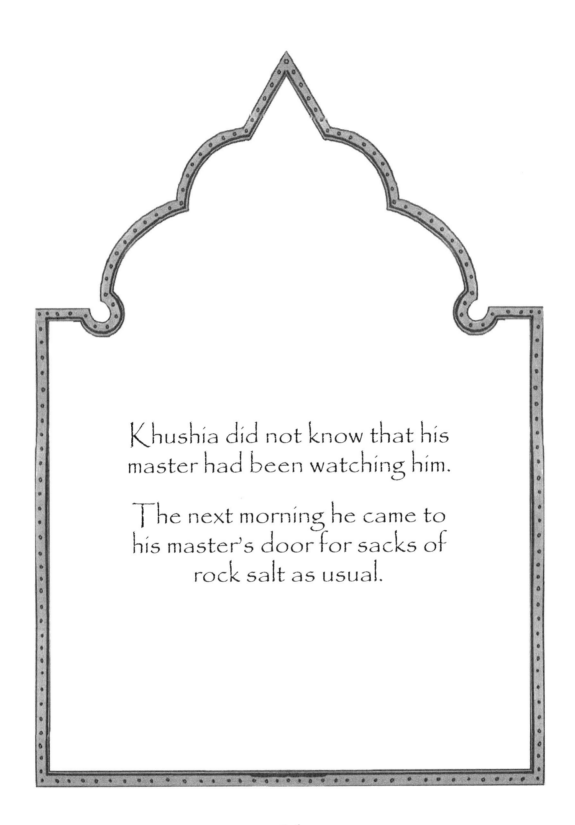

Khushia did not know that his master had been watching him.

The next morning he came to his master's door for sacks of rock salt as usual.

The merchant brought two sacks as he had always done and placed them on Khushia's back. Khushia started to walk towards the stream and the merchant followed him again at a distance.

Fearlessly plunging into the deep water had become second nature to Khushia. In fact, he had started to enjoy going through the deep waters.

This morning, as usual, Khushia looked for the deep waters and went straight into the depths. He swam leisurely for a while.

Khushia decided to swim to the other side of the stream so to resume his journey. He tried to climb up on the grassy land, but his hoof slipped.

He tried again and again, but again he slipped back into the water.

He quickly became tired and so gave up and sat in the water, panting.

Khushia looked up hopelessly.

The merchant was waiting for him nearby. Instead of sacks of salt, the merchant had placed sacks of cotton on Khushia's back. The cotton had absorbed the water and the sacks had become extremely heavy.

That was the reason why Khushia could not get out of the water.

After a while, the merchant pushed the sacks away from Khushia's back and pulled him out of the water.

Khushia's legs were trembling with weakness, he sank on the dry ground.

The merchant felt sorry for him; he sat down near Khushia, gently moving his hand over his head and back.

For the first time in a long while, Khushia felt happy. He knew his master had forgiven him for his dirty trick.

The merchant took Khushia home. Although he had taught Khushia a good lesson, Khushia had also opened the eyes of the merchant to the fact that masters should always treat their animals with love and care.

The merchant dealt kindly with Khushia for the rest of his life.

He made it his life's duty to teach all the other merchants in the village how to treat their animals with love and care.

From then on, Khushia had no worries in his life. He roamed the open streets and the footpaths of the village at leisure. When ever he wished, he came back to the loving protection of his master, the merchant.

Now Khushia was *Khushia* in the real sense of the word.

Khushia.

A happy donkey!

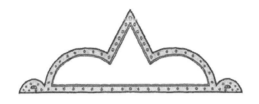

Did you like the story? Good, if you did!

Now, I would like to ask you some questions
– see if you can answer them.

Have you got a pet? If you do, what do you call it?

Is your pet an animal, a bird, a reptile or an insect?

How do you show that you love and care for your pet?

What does the NSPCC and RSPCA stand for?

Don't worry if you don't know, you can ask your mummy or daddy or your teacher to help you.

See you soon!

Printed in Great Britain
by Amazon

80565954R00032